HELPING YOUR BRAND-NEW READER

Here's how to make first-time reading easy and fun:

▶ Read the introduction at the beginning of the book aloud. Look through the pictures together so that your child can see what happens in the story before reading the words.

▶ Read the first page to your child, placing your finger under each word.

▶ Let your child touch the words and read the rest of the story. Give him or her time to figure out each new word.

▶ If your child gets stuck on a word, you might say, *"Try something. Look at the picture. What would make sense?"*

▶ If your child is still stuck, supply the right word. This will allow him or her to continue to read and enjoy the story. You might say, *"Could this word be 'ball'?"*

▶ Always praise your child. Praise what he or she reads correctly, and praise good tries too.

▶ Give your child lots of chances to read the story again and again. The more your child reads, the more confident he or she will become.

▶ Have fun!

Text copyright © 2001 by David Martin
Illustrations copyright © 2001 by Frank Remkiewicz

All rights reserved.

First edition 2001

Library of Congress Cataloging-in-Publication Data
is available.

Library of Congress Catalog Card Number 00-047405

ISBN 0-7636-1326-6

2 4 6 8 10 9 7 5 3 1

Printed in Hong Kong

This book was typeset in Letraset Arta.
The illustrations were done in watercolor and ink.

Candlewick Press
2067 Massachusetts Avenue
Cambridge, Massachusetts 02140

PIGGY AND DAD

CANDLEWICK PRESS
CAMBRIDGE, MASSACHUSETTS

David Martin ILLUSTRATED BY **Frank Remkiewicz**

Contents

PIGGY'S SANDWICH

Introduction

This story is called *Piggy's Sandwich*. It's about how Dad and Piggy make sandwiches for themselves, but then Piggy eats Dad's sandwich too.

Dad makes a sandwich.

Piggy makes a sandwich too.

Dad eats his sandwich.

Piggy eats his sandwich too.

Dad makes another sandwich.

Piggy makes another sandwich too.

Piggy eats his sandwich.

Piggy eats Dad's sandwich too.

PIGGY'S PICTURES

Introduction

This story is called *Piggy's Pictures.*
It's about how Piggy draws pictures and
Dad writes the words to go with the pictures.

Piggy draws a house.

Dad writes "house."

Piggy draws a clown.

Dad writes "clown."

Piggy draws a dinosaur.

Dad writes "dinosaur."

Piggy draws a heart.

Dad writes "Dad loves Piggy."

PIGGY'S BATH

Introduction

This story is called *Piggy's Bath*.
It's about all the things Piggy gets before he takes a bath, and then what Dad has to get.

Piggy gets a boat.

Piggy gets a duck.

Piggy gets a ball.

Piggy gets a cup.

Piggy gets goggles.

Piggy gets in the bathtub.

Splash!

Dad gets a mop.

PIGGY'S BEDTIME

Introduction

This story is called *Piggy's Bedtime.*
It's about the things Piggy and Dad do
before Piggy goes to sleep.

Piggy gets in bed.

Dad gets in bed.

Dad reads to Piggy.

Piggy reads to Dad.

Dad kisses Piggy good night.

Piggy kisses Dad good night.

Dad and Piggy smile.

PILLOW FIGHT!